My Brother John

For Catherine
K.N.

For John, Luke and Peter
K.C.

My Brother J·O·H·N

KRISTINE CHURCH

illustrated by
KILMENY NILAND

Tambourine Books · New York

Library of Congress Cataloging in Publication Data
Church, Kristine. My brother John/by Kristine Church;
illustrated by Kilmeny Niland. p. cm.
SUMMARY: A younger sister describes her almost
fearless, older brother.
ISBN 0-688-10800-8 — ISBN 0-688-10801-6 (lib. bdg.)
[1. Brothers and sisters — Fiction. 2. Courage — Fiction.
3. Fear — Fiction.] I. Niland, Kilmeny, ill.
II. Title. PZ7.C4704My 1991 [E] — dc20
90-25868 CIP AC

My brother John
is older and bigger than I am.

My brother John
is fearless and brave.

At night when my bedroom is dark,
my brother John goes into it looking very scary and fierce.
He frightens away all the ghosts and greebies.
Even the ones under my bed.

Every last one.

Out the window they go.

When John tells me it's all clear,
I go in and get into bed.

My brother John
is fearless and brave.
Before I have my bath at night,
he puts on his snorkel and flippers.

With a very scary face
he dives right to the bottom of the bathtub.
He fights off all the sharks and sea monsters
and squashes them down the drain.

When all is clear
I go in and take a bath.

My brother John
is fearless and brave.
When I go to our secret treehouse,
he goes up the ladder first.
He puts on his magic red cape and
calls for a jar of water.
Up into the treehouse goes
my brother John.

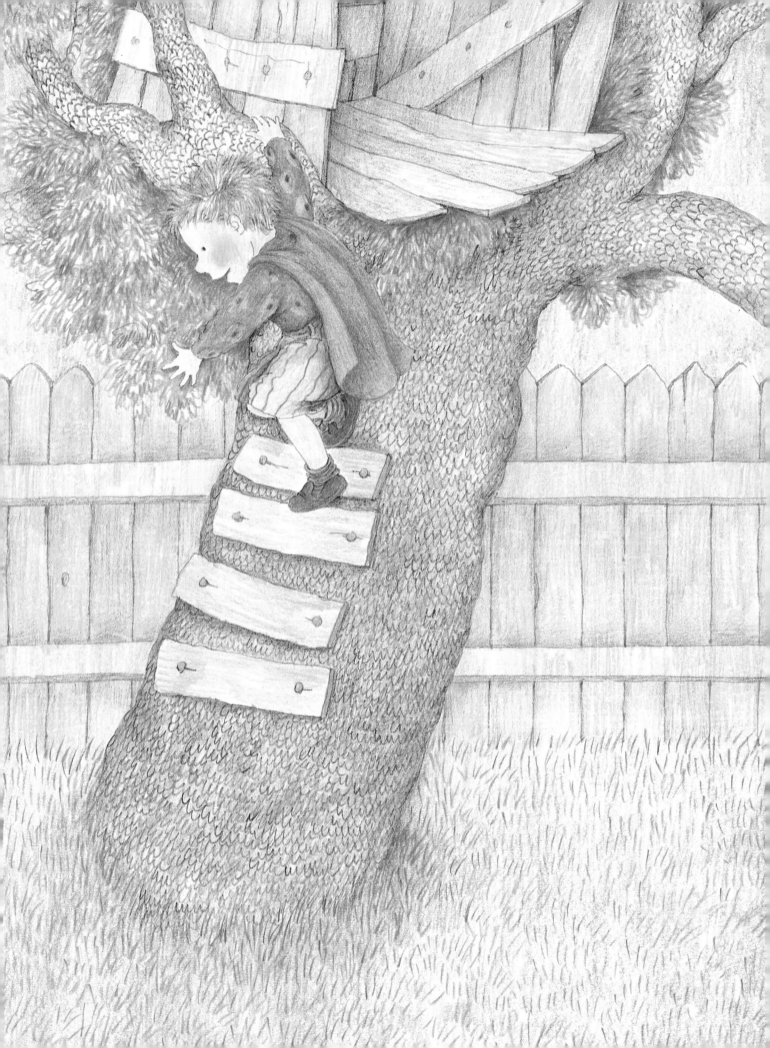

Then he fights all the fire-breathing dragons
until they fly away.

Even the little ones.

When all is safe
I go up into the treehouse.

My brother John
is older and bigger than I am.
My brother John
is fearless and brave except when it comes to . . .

GREEN FROGS.

He turns a funny color.

"Put on your fierce and scary face!"
I yell to my brother John.
But it doesn't help.
"Put on your snorkel and flippers!"
I yell to my brother John.
But they don't help either
and his eyes start to bulge.
"Quick! Get your magic cape and jar of water!"
I yell to my brother John.

But he looks a bit silly
standing there with all that stuff on,
and he's still a funny color.

So I go over and pick up the fat green frog.
I pat him on his squishy, green back
and take him way down to the back of the house.
I hide him very carefully in the leaves
where John can't see him.
My brother John
is fearless and brave with just about everything . . .

except
GREEN FROGS.